MAXIE

BY MILDRED KANTROWITZ
PICTURES BY EMILY A. McCULLY

Parents' Magazine Press • New York

To my mother who was necessary to begin with

MAXIE lived in three small rooms
on the top floor of an old brownstone
house on Orange Street.
She had lived there for many years,
and every day was the same for Maxie.
Every morning, seven days a week,
every morning at exactly seven o'clock,
Maxie raised the shades on her three
front windows.
Every morning at exactly 7:10,
Maxie's large, orange cat jumped up
onto the middle windowsill
and sprawled there in the morning sun.

At 7:20, if you were watching Maxie's back
window, you could see her raise the shade
to the very top.
Then she uncovered a bird cage. On the perch
inside the cage was a yellow canary. He was
waiting for his water dish to be filled, and
it always was, if you were still watching,
at 7:22.

At 8:15 every morning, Maxie's door opened
with a tired squeak.
Maxie's old, leather slippers made slapping
sounds as she walked down the four flights
of uncarpeted stairs to the front door.
Outside the front door were the bottles of milk
in a container. Maxie always tried to hold
the door open with her left foot while she
reached out to get her milk.
But every morning it was just a little too far
for her to reach. The door always banged shut
and locked behind her.

So, at 8:20 every morning, Maxie rang the bell marked "Superintendent." The superintendent, whose name was Arthur, would open the door for Maxie and let her in with her milk.

Only Maxie and the man at the grocery store knew
what she ate for breakfast, but everyone knew
she drank tea. At 8:45 every morning, they could
hear the whistling of her tea kettle.
How Maxie loved that whistle! She loved it so much
that she let it sing out for one full minute.
Dogs howled, cats whined and babies bawled, but
everyone knew that when the whistle stopped, it
would be 8:46. And it always was.

The mailman knew more about Maxie than anyone else did.
He knew that she had a sister in Chicago who sent her
a Christmas card every year. He also knew when Maxie
planted the flowers in her window boxes because every
spring he delivered her seed catalog. Then a few weeks
later he delivered packets of seeds.

Every morning at nine o'clock, Maxie walked down the stairs
for the second time in her leather slippers. She went
outside and put her small bag of garbage in the pail
on the front stoop.
Then she came back in and waited for the mailman. She walked
slowly past him in the hall, watching him put mail in the
slots for the other people who lived in the house.

Then she climbed the four flights
of stairs again, resting at each
landing. When she got to the top,
Maxie went into her apartment,
and the door closed after her
with the same tired squeak.

One afternoon at 1:05, just as she did every afternoon at 1:05, Maxie moved the bird cage with the yellow bird in it to the front windows. It was shady and cool there now.

The large, orange cat moved
to the back window and
sprawled there, soaking up
the sun that matched the
color of his fur.

"You're perfectly happy just lying there, day
after day," Maxie said to the cat. "All you
ever want to do is move from one windowsill
to the other and watch the world go by.
You don't need anyone, and no one really
needs you. But you don't seem to care."
Maxie turned away from the window.
"I care," she said sadly. "I'm not a cat.
But I might as well be."
Maxie felt very tired, and she went to bed.
That was Monday.

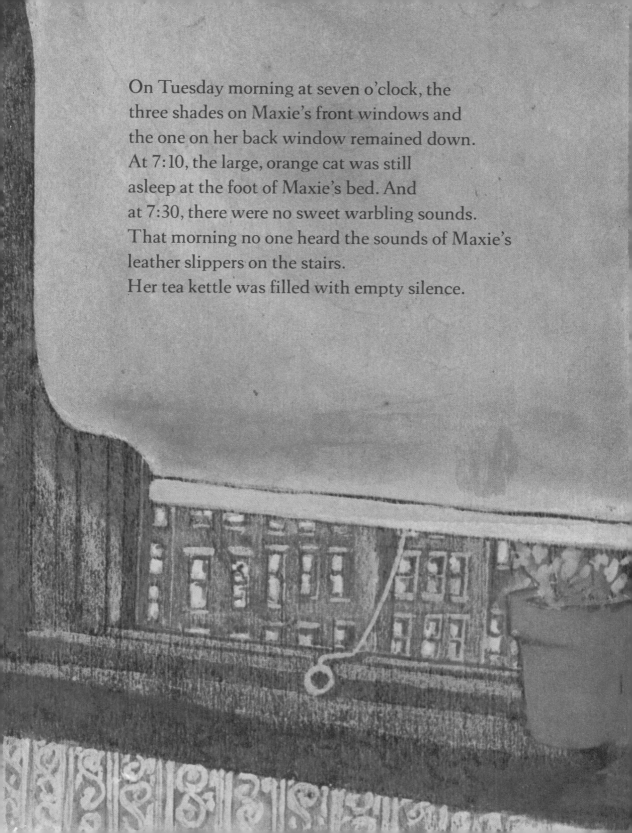

On Tuesday morning at seven o'clock, the
three shades on Maxie's front windows and
the one on her back window remained down.
At 7:10, the large, orange cat was still
asleep at the foot of Maxie's bed. And
at 7:30, there were no sweet warbling sounds.
That morning no one heard the sounds of Maxie's
leather slippers on the stairs.
Her tea kettle was filled with empty silence.

At nine o'clock, the
mailman came with the
daily mail. He had a
seed catalog for Maxie
and he waited for her
to come down the stairs.
Since she didn't come
and this was most
unusual, he decided
to deliver the catalog
to her door.

He climbed the four
flights of stairs.
He knocked and waited.
There was no sign
of Maxie.

At 9:03, Mr. Turkle who lived on the third floor
came hurrying up the stairs.
At 9:05, Mr. and Mrs. Moorehouse
got there from across the street.
At 9:07, Mrs. Trueheart came
over from next door.
Susie Smith came up at 9:10
with her twin brothers.

Five members of the family on the second floor
made it up by 9:13.
Then came Arthur, the superintendent.
By 9:17, there were seventeen people, three dogs
and two cats, all waiting for Maxie to open
the door.

And when she didn't they all went in.
They found Maxie in bed.
More people came up the stairs and someone called
a doctor. By the time he got there, there were
forty-two grown-ups and eleven children in Maxie's
small living room.

When the doctor came out of Maxie's bedroom he shook his head sadly. "Maxie isn't really sick," he said. "She's lonely. She doesn't feel loved. She doesn't feel that anyone needs her."
No one said anything for a minute. Then suddenly Mrs. Trueheart got up and walked right past the doctor and into the bedroom. "Maxie!" she shouted angrily, "you let me down. You and that warbling bird let me down!

"Every morning I wake up when I hear that bird. Then it's my job to wake my husband. He has the morning shift at the corner diner and he's still asleep. Why, there must be at least seventy-five people at that diner right now, waiting for their breakfasts. They'll all have to go to work on empty stomachs — all because of you and that yellow bird!"

Everyone else crowded into the bedroom. Maxie sat
up in bed and listened to what they had to say.
"I couldn't go to school this morning," Susie Smith
said. "I missed my bus because I didn't hear your
tea kettle whistle."

"The school bus never came this morning," said Mr. Turkle who drove the bus. "I didn't wake up in time. I never heard Sarah Sharpe's footsteps on my ceiling."

Sarah Sharpe was a nurse who lived just above Mr. Turkle. There were a lot of people waiting for her right now at the hospital. She always got up when she heard Maxie's door squeak.

Mr. and Mrs. Moorehouse both had very important jobs
but they had missed their train that morning. Their
alarm clock was Maxie's window shade.
Arthur said he hadn't swept the front steps that
morning. He overslept because Maxie didn't ring his
bell. He hoped no one would complain.
They all talked about it and decided that there must
be about four hundred people who needed Maxie — or who
needed someone else who needed Maxie — every morning.

Maxie smiled. She got out of bed and made
a pot of tea. In fact, she made five pots
of tea.
Each time the kettle whistled, dogs howled,
cats whined and babies bawled.
Maxie listened and thought about how many people
were being touched by these sounds — her sounds.
By 9:45 that morning, Maxie had served tea
to everybody, and she was so pleased.